THICK

I did it.
I know I told you that
when you were here, Ms. Lawson,
but I want to say it again.
I did it.
I pulled the trigger.
I shot someone.
Dead.

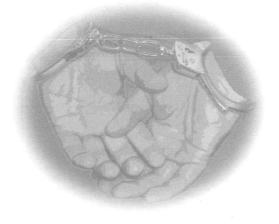

Books by Colin Neenan

Idiot!

Live a Little
In Your Dreams

THICK

COLIN NEENAN

Brown Barn Books
Weston, Connecticut

Brown Barn Books
A division of Pictures of Record, Inc.
119 Kettle Creek Road, Weston, CT 06883, U.S.A.
www.brownbarnbooks.com

Thick

Original paperback edition

10 9 8 7 6 5 4

Library of Congress Control Number 2005935278

ISBN: 0-9746481-9-1
     978-0-9746481-9-4

Neenan, Colin
THICK

Printed in the United States of America

to
Cadence and Alix

Acknowledgments

There are a lot of people who made this a better book, and I'd like to write a brief thank you to some of them right here.

To Jodi Netting and Polly Dyer, thank you for your support and your lessons in how to live life.

To Kate Dickstein, reading specialist, and Margery Fisher, librarian, thank you for your wise comments and suggestions.

To Elizabeth Bennett, thank you for being a wonderful friend, a kind reader, and an irrepressible, but gentle, editor.

And to Nancy Hammerslough, my publisher, editor, and friend, thank you for all your help as well as your faith in *THICK*.

ONE

I did it.

I know I told you that when you were here, Ms. Lawson, but I want to say it again.

I did it.

I pulled the trigger.

I shot someone.

Dead.

I killed someone. Nothing is going to change that. I pulled the trigger, and the gun went off, bang! It was loud, I was surprised at how loud a gun was, like someone wants to hurt your ears.

And then there was blood. I knew there would be a lot of blood, just like in the movies. But this was real blood. Real blood with a real blood smell.

I did not know blood would smell.

TWO

I don't know how to do this, Ms. Lawson.

You said to start at the beginning. But every time I try, all I can do is think about the end. All I can do is hear the shot. And see the blood.

I feel bad because you are a very nice lady, Ms. Lawson. I wish the other men in the cell here did not whistle and shout those things at you yesterday when you came to talk to me. You said you are used to it, but I do not think a lady should have to get used to that. Even when they are pretty, like you.

I would not come back here, if I were you. I told Hope not to come back. Hope is my sister, I don't remember if I told you her name. She does not listen to me, Hope doesn't, partly because she is eighteen and I am only seventeen, but also because she is a lot smarter than I am. I wish she would not come here, though. She comes to see me and she cries. I tell her it is not too bad in here, but she cries anyway.

"Listen to Ms. Lawson, Nick. She's your lawyer," Hope tells me, over and over, like I'm going to forget.

I don't think I need a lawyer. I'm not innocent, I know that and you know that and everyone should know that. I am guilty.

Why does someone who is guilty need a lawyer?

THREE

Please don't think I want to go to prison. I do not want to go to prison. The men here say it is worse than where I am right now, which is a holding cell while I wait for my trial. There are fifteen of us in this cell, I have counted. And we have a toilet right out in the open, so you have to pee and even do the other thing with everyone there. There's not even a toilet seat. I don't understand why we cannot have a toilet seat.

FOUR

Ms. Lawson, before you get mad at me because I'm not doing this right, you need to understand something.

I'm stupid.

Mrs. Brown would be mad, hearing me say that, but Mrs. Brown teaches special education, which means she has to say you are smart even if you really aren't. What is funny about Mrs. Brown is I think she really doesn't think we are stupid. She's wrong, but still, it is nice.

There are mostly just dumb kids in Mrs. Brown's classes, and I am about the dumbest. I'm not retarded, if that's what you think. Brad Thornton calls me a retard, but I'm not. Brad is in Mrs. Brown's class, and he calls me a retard, but that's just because he's mean. My dad calls me Thick, sometimes, instead of Nick, which is my real name. Thick is another word for stupid, and Dad calls me Thick when he's in a really mean mood, but he knows I'm not retarded. I'm just not good at learning. Things take me longer, and they don't stick as well. But I look pretty much like everyone else in high school, only bigger. I have always been big for my age, and a little heavy. I look like I should play football. Dad made me play in the sixth grade, but I didn't like trying to push people around and tackle them, and sometimes when people hit me it would hurt. We lost our last game by a lot. I remember it was cold and the ground hurt when you fell down, and when we got home Dad started drinking beer and told Mom I was too stupid to play football. I heard him say it and went into the room I shared with Hope and cried. Mom came in and sat beside me on the bed and put her arm around me.

"Nicky, look at me," Mom said. She always called me Nicky. At least that is all I can remember her calling me. She has been gone for three years now, but I think she always called me Nicky. "Look at me," she said again.

I looked at her smiling into my face. Mom had a way of looking at you that made you believe she really liked being with you.

"Are you mean?" she asked. "Are you mean to people?"

I didn't understand why she was asking, but I shook my head. "No."

Mom wiped the tears off my cheeks. "Then you are not stupid, Nicky. If you are not mean, you are not stupid. Because only mean people are stupid. Do you understand? Only mean people are stupid, and that's the truth."

I believed Mom, that only mean people are stupid, and it really did make me feel better. Sometimes I even still believe her. A part of me, at least.

But the rest of me knows I am just plain dumb.

Mrs. Brown works with me with writing, though. She makes writing not so awful because she helps me fix my mistakes. She's very good at helping, she helps everyone fix their mistakes without making them feel stupid. Some teachers think she cheats for us, that she gives us too much help, but how can you give someone too much help? Mrs. Brown gets mad when she hears other teachers say this. She cleans up her desk when she gets mad. Throws things in the filing cabinet. "Do they WANT to torture you? Is that their goal, to make you hate coming here?" She means coming to school. Mrs. Brown tries to help us want to come to school. She has a real welcome mat outside her classroom. It is made of thick straw and says WELCOME in large, brown letters. It looks like something people in big houses would put outside their front doors, but Mrs. Brown has it right outside her classroom because she wants us to like school. I still do not like it because school is no fun when you are stupid.

But I like the welcome mat.

FIVE

Maybe the beginning starts with Alice. Who I saw the very first time on my first day at Joe's. And who I kind of fell in love with.

Joe's is a diner. A lawyer like you probably mostly goes to restaurants. I know there are lots of restaurants in the rest of Connecticut, but in Bridgetown we have mostly diners.

Joe's is named after Joe Daniels, who owns the diner. My dad knew Mr. Daniels from school and bought him a drink at McCann's one night and asked him if he could use a hard worker like his son and Mr. Daniels said sure.

That was what Dad said when he got home that night, anyway. He was drunk but he was happy so it was OK. Sometimes Dad could be fun when he was drunk, he could laugh and tell jokes that were not mean. That night he was very happy because he thought he had gotten me the job at Joe's. He said I needed to go there the

11

next day after school. I was very nervous, hearing about the job, and I did not want to go by myself, but I knew not to say anything because when he was drunk, Dad's good mood could change into a bad mood really fast.

The next day I walked straight from school to Joe's. My legs were shaking, I was so scared. I don't like to say this, but I was even ready to cry. Ever since I was little, I've always been too ready to cry. Which looks pretty silly, considering I'm so big.

I didn't cry walking to Joe's, but I had to work hard not to. Dad said to walk in the back door, and I walked around to the back of Joe's, but all I saw were weeds covered with paper cups and plastic bags and other garbage. I walked through the weeds and found the back door on the other side of the building. The door opened to the kitchen, where a man was using a spatula to turn over burgers smoking on the grill. He didn't see me, and I was afraid to talk to him, so I kept walking and found Mr. Daniels in a little office. He was writing numbers in a big green book with thin lines.

"Can I help you?" he asked, when he finally looked up. His beard made him look really serious.

"I'm Nick," I said. But by the way he was looking at me, I could tell this wasn't enough.

"Nick Laden," I said. "You know my dad?"

Mr. Daniels nodded. "I saw Ben last night, yeah."

I coughed. "He said he talked to you?"

Mr. Daniels did not stop looking at me. "About what?" he asked.

I knew then what had happened. Dad had been drunk. Dad had been drunk and didn't really get me the job. He wanted to get me the job, and he may have even bought Mr. Daniels a drink, but instead of getting me the job Dad just convinced himself that he had gotten me the job. I'd seen it before. Hope says when Dad gets really drunk, he can't always tell the difference between what happened and what he wanted to have happened.

One thing was for sure: Mr. Daniels had not offered me a job like Dad had said he did.

"I—I—I—" I don't stutter a lot, except when I feel really stupid. "I—I—I'm sorry to bother you, sir." I was backing up, looking down at my fat fingers that I did not know what to do with. I backed into one of those yellow janitorial buckets on wheels and knocked over the mop that was standing up in it. "I'm sorry," I said, swinging around, trying to grab the mop. It was falling, though, so instead of grabbing it, my hand knocked it down, the end of the handle slamming down on the toes of someone who was standing outside the office.

That was how I met Alice.

"Ow," she said.

SIX

I could tell it hurt, really hurt, but Alice was nice about it, pretending it was no big deal.

"I'm really, I—I—I—" I kept looking down at her toes. "I'm really sorry."

Alice laughed and reached over and pushed her finger into my cheek. "Boy, do you know how to blush," she said.

"I'm really sorry," I said, again.

"About what? Blushing?"

"No," I said, pointing to her toe. "I'm sorry about—"

"I know, I know," Alice said. "I was teasing you."

"Oh. Oh!" And then I finally looked at her, looked at Alice's face.

And kind of fell in love.

I don't like admitting that. I know it sounds stupid, to fall in love with someone by looking at them, but it's not as bad as some people might think.

See, Alice is not pretty. I don't mean that in a bad away, I just mean that most times when guys fall in love right away, it's because of how pretty the girl is. Like Suzie Knowlton in Mrs. Brown's class. Suzie's in my class with Mrs. Brown, and just about every guy in the class is in love with Suzie and her blond hair and her tight shirts. Sometimes I have to try not to look her, she's so pretty.

But Alice is not like that. Not right away, anyway. Alice is almost fat. And her skin isn't great and her hair is sort of all over the place.

So I didn't know for a long time why I kind of fell in love, like I said. It took me awhile to realize that it had to do with her face being able to smile all at the same time. I liked that, liked the way she could all the way smile even though I had just bashed her toes with a mop handle. So I guess she was pretty that way, with her face making that all-the-way smile.

Alice smiled at me and looked at Mr. Daniels. "Is this the new dishwasher?" she asked.

And that was how Alice got me the job Dad thought he had gotten for me.

SEVEN

Mr. Daniels said I could start right away, and the three of us walked back into the dishwashing place. No wonder Mr. Daniels hired me. There were dirty dishes stacked up everywhere, and two deep sinks were full of dirty pots and pans, and everything smelled like garbage left out in the rain.

But the scariest thing was the dishwashing machine. It was a dull steel box the size of a car. And when Mr. Daniels pushed the buttons to turn it on, it was so loud it sounded angry and you had to yell if you wanted someone to hear you.

Mr. Daniels had Alice show me how to load the trays. I think Alice could tell I was stupid because she really took her time, showing me how to separate the silverware into knives and spoons and forks.

"Think you've got it now?" she asked, finally, when Mr. Daniels came back and yelled at her. Alice was a waitress, and she was wasting so much time showing me how to load the trays for the dishwasher that her customers were getting hungry.

Of course, I forgot everything as soon as Alice left. That is the way it always works with me. Mrs. Brown can stand there beside me and I can do all the math problems. But the second she walks away, I forget my times tables.

The first couple of trays that went through the dishwasher were all wrong, the plates not tilted the way they need to be tilted to get clean.

"What the hell?"

I was working on another tray when a skinny guy with a pointy mustache walked over and held in front of my face a plate with red splotches all over it.

"Does this look clean to you?" he asked.

"I—I—I—No," I said.

"Yeah, well, I—I—I—think you should clean it again. And get it right this time."

That was how I met Sam Harding.

Who I really wish I'd never in my life met.

EIGHT

Some of the other prisoners are laughing at me for writing this.

Everyone here seems older than I am. They aren't like the guys at school, but seem like men. Three of them are skinheads. Mrs. Brown told us about skinheads. She said they are people who shave their heads and stick together, hating people. There are some skinheads at school, but the skinheads at school aren't as big and tattooed as the three here in our cell.

The shortest skinhead came up and asked me what I was doing, writing in this notebook, and when I said that my lawyer wants me to write everything down, he and his two skinhead friends started laughing.

"How f---ing stupid can you get?" one of them said.

"Pretty f---ing stupid," the tallest one told him. He had a big black spider tattooed on the back of his bald head. I thought it was real when I first saw it, and

I was glad it wasn't because it was huge and sat right on the knobby thing on the back of his head.

The three men told me lawyers *always* want you to write everything down. It makes their job easier. It means they don't need to talk to us. They don't need to look at us. They don't need to smell us.

"You think that f---ing lawyer lady wants to HELP you?" the shortest one said, standing over me. He was flexing his muscles and looked like I was annoying him, just sitting there.

I *did* think you wanted to help me. I hope I'm not writing this because you don't like the way it smells in here. But I don't blame you, the smell is bad. I wanted to hold my nose when I first got here, but now I've gotten used to it.

I am not sure that is a good thing.

NINE

It was dark and cold, walking home after work that first day. We live in an old house on Muir, just behind the railroad tracks, where the houses are crowded together with just an alley between them. I could tell from two houses away that Dad was in a bad mood. I could tell because the only light on in the house was the blue flickering glow from the television in the living room. When Dad was angry about something, he liked to sit in the dark.

I was quiet, letting myself in through the side door, by the kitchen.

"*Hope*?" Dad called.

"No, it's just me, Dad," I called back to him.

"Well, for once in your life you can count your blessings you're you," he muttered, loud enough for me to hear, even though I couldn't tell if he wanted me to.

I walked through the dark to turn on the light over the stove. It was the only light that was safe to turn on when Dad was sitting in the dark because the overhead light, the bathroom light, and the hallway light all spilled into the living room. When Dad was sitting in the dark he would explode if you started shining lights.

I turned on the light over the stove and looked in the old, chipped sink. In the sink were eight beer cans. Eight was bad. Dad worked the 6 to 3 shift at the chemical factory all the way over on Patterson. It took awhile for him to get home since he had to take two buses. It was only 5:30, so he'd drunk eight beers in less than two hours, which was bad. And since he left the cans in the sink, he didn't care what Hope thought, which meant he had to be good and mad about something.

"Where the hell's your sister?" he hollered from the living room.

A lot of times Dad got mad if I tried to answer his questions. The same way he got really annoyed at me for being stupid, as if I was trying to do it on purpose.

"I'll get dinner started," I said. Maybe that was the problem. Maybe Dad was hungry and dinner was not ready when he got home.

I washed out the beer cans and took them outside to the blue recycling bin and mixed them up with the cans already out there. If Hope didn't know Dad had had so much beer, and I could feed Dad before Hope got home, maybe all hell would not break loose.

Unfortunately, when I stood up from stirring around the cans in the recycling bin, Hope was standing there, looking at me.

"How many?" she asked.

TEN

I need to stop and tell you about Hope. You know she is a senior in high school, only a year older than me, but most people find it hard to believe. Hope got a lot older the night Mom died.

It was three years ago. To understand Hope, you have to know what happened three years ago, just before Christmas.

Hope was in the ninth grade and I was still in middle school. When I woke up the morning of Christmas Eve, the house was very quiet but freezing. When I went out to the living room, I found out why—someone had smashed our Christmas tree right through the living room window. Hardly anything can wake me up, when I'm asleep, but I couldn't believe I didn't hear the Christmas tree going through the living room window.

While I was standing there, looking at the Christmas tree outside on the bushes, Hope came up from the basement. She had found some clear plastic and used the staple gun to stick up the plastic to cover the hole where the window had been. Then she went out and dragged the tree back inside and got me to help her stand it back up again. She even went back outside and picked up the big pieces of broken ornaments, mostly shiny pieces of thin glass.

Mom and Dad were both gone, so Hope kind of took over. She got together all the dirty clothes and we walked to the Laundromat and washed everything. When we got home, Hope had me wash the kitchen floor while she folded laundry. Dad hated Christmas music, but since he was gone we were able to play Christmas carols on Mom's clock radio.

Hope made spaghetti and meatballs, my favorite, for dinner. But when we sat down to eat, someone knocked on the door. It was a policeman and a police woman. Dad must have done something. That was what I thought. Not very often, but sometimes Dad would hit someone or throw something and the police would take him to jail. And then the police would come to the house, and Mom would go down to the police station.

So I wasn't that scared when the police knocked on the door and asked to come inside. Hope told me to do the dishes. I said we hadn't eaten yet, but she said to wash the pots and clean the sink.

I started washing the big spaghetti pot but hadn't gotten very far when I heard Hope scream in the living room. It was the strangest scream I'd ever heard, like an animal caught in the jaws of a horrible trap.

I spilled water all over the floor, running out of the kitchen and into the living room. The police woman was holding Hope tightly.

"Noooooooooooooooooooooooooo!"

It was the saddest sound, and it was pouring out of Hope. I didn't know what was happening, but I started to cry, feeling sorry for Hope. And scared for me.

The policeman stood in my way. He didn't push me, but he held out his arms at either side and kind of swept me back into the kitchen. I could hear Hope crying and wanted to see her, to do something, but I think maybe the policeman was worried Hope and I would just make each other worse.

Dad came home a little while later, and Hope stopped crying and came into the kitchen. She made me eat dinner while the two police officers talked quietly to Dad. She didn't eat, but she watched me eat.

"Mom got hit by a car," she said softly, and I could see her eyes filling up with tears as she looked at me. "She's dead."

I didn't cry. I don't know what you're supposed to do when you find out your mother is dead, but I just sat there hugging myself because I felt so cold. I felt really cold and went and climbed into bed with my clothes on and pulled the covers up tight to my chin and shut my eyes and didn't move.

I don't remember very much about the funeral, but I remember the day after we found out Mom was dead, Dad took me hiking. When we were little, Dad would take me and Hope hiking. I don't like to brag, but I'm a very good hiker. I'm not bragging a lot because all you have to do to be a good hiker is to walk through the woods and like it. I love hiking, maybe partly because I'm so good at it. Even Dad thought I was a good hiker because I didn't get tired or complain like Hope sometimes did.

We didn't hike as much when I got older and got on Dad's nerves more easily, but I remember the day after Mom died, Dad took me. It was very cold. Dad walked fast, which I like. I also like walking slow or even just standing, surrounded by trees. The ground did not smell a lot that day, because it was so cold, but the wind made the branches wave a slow hello. Or good-bye, maybe. This is silly, but I remember looking up at some of the highest branches and thinking Mom had found a way to wave good-bye.

ELEVEN

Anyway, now it was three years later, and Hope caught me hiding the beer cans in the recycling bin.

"How many?" she asked, "and don't lie."

"Three," I said.

Hope threw her hands up in the air. "Why do you lie for him?"

I don't, I wanted to tell her. *I lie for you.* Because no matter how smart Hope is, she does not see what I see, doesn't know what I know. I know that Dad hurts her. Hope is tough and can stand up to Dad and survive, but I know the words Dad uses are like little cuts all over her. And I knew one day she was just not going to be tough enough anymore.

And then what?

TWELVE

Hope made the door sound like thunder when she slammed it.

"What the f--- are you doing, Nick?" Dad screamed.

"It's not Nick!" Hope screamed back.

I wanted to run. When I was little and Mom and Dad fought, I used to go to the bathroom and run water in the bathtub. When it got really loud, I'd hum to myself, staring at the water rushing out of the faucet.

Now I wanted to just run as far as my legs would carry me.

"Hope?" Dad charged into the kitchen, holding a sheet of paper in his fist. "What is this, little girl? Just what the hell is this?" He flung the paper. On its own, it drifted to the floor, "*We have received your application*? They have received your f---ing application?"

Hope reached over and flicked on the overhead light. "What's your point?"

"My point? I'll give you my point, little girl."

"The name is Hope."

"My point is we talked about this. My point is I told you we can't afford college."

"I'll get a scholarship."

"Forget it. I told you, you're not going. Do you hear me? You are not going."

"I'm going," she said. "And I'm taking Nick with me."

My heart jumped up. I had heard about Hope going to college, I knew she wanted to go to college, but I had never heard that she wanted to take me with her.

Dad charged toward Hope. I thought he was going to do it, I thought this time he was really going to do it, he was going to hit her. Instead he put his face right up next to her face. "I said no."

Hope did not move, did not blink, did not back down. "I'm going."

Dad leaned even closer and whispered. "Over – my – dead – body."

Did Hope mean it?

Was she really going to take me with her to college? How could she? What would we do?

Hope slammed the door when she left, and Dad just kept cursing as he opened the refrigerator for another beer and took it back into the living room.

I was scared to leave, but I really wanted to talk to Hope. Real quiet, I grabbed my jacket and opened the door. Outside it was cold but I felt like I could breathe again. I walked slowly across our backyard.

Behind our house are railroad tracks. We have a small little backyard, and then there is a line of trees, and then a chain link fence that comes up to my chest. Hope taught me how to stick one sneaker into the chain link and hop over, but she also warned me to hold on tight to the fence, and this is why. On the other side of the fence the ground slants down steep to the top of a wall. The wall is about ten feet high and right down at the bottom of the wall are the railroad tracks.

"If you fall off the wall, you'll die," Hope warned me, the very first time she took me to the fence and showed me how to climb over it.

Climbing over now, I held on tight to the top of the fence, just like Hope taught me.

I knew Hope liked to come watch the train speeding toward New York City, and I was hoping I would find her there now, in the dark.

"Hope?" I called, moving slowly, not able to see much. "*Hope*?"

I moved slowly and reached the top of the wall. Hope was not there, but I sat down and dangled my legs off the top of the wall. I had a feeling it was a dream of Hope's to be one of those people who rode the train every day to an important job.

And I knew that dream started with college.

Even if she didn't take me with her, Hope needed to go to college.

And sitting there in the dark, I was scared because I didn't know if Dad could stop her.

THIRTEEN

I didn't know if Dad could stop Hope. But I knew somebody who would know.

"Mrs. Brown, can I ask you something?" It was almost the end of seventh period. I had done all my homework a long time ago, but I waited until Brad Thornton got up and waited by the door for the bell to ring.

Brad is the last person I need to tell you about, Ms. Lawson.

Brad is smart, at least smart compared to the rest of us in Mrs. Brown's class. And he likes to make fun of the rest of us who aren't as smart as he is.

He's especially good at making fun of me, and this is why.

Brad Thornton lives across the street from McCann's. That's the bar where my dad drinks when he does not drink at home. Since Mr. McCann knew

Brad from the neighborhood, he would let Brad work in the bar, cleaning up and washing glasses and running errands for customers. Dad liked Brad and sometimes when he would come home from McCann's he would ask me why I wasn't funny like Brad or smart like Brad. Sometimes Dad would even tell Brad about stupid things I had done, and then Brad would have fun, telling everyone at school.

So I did not want Brad hearing what I wanted to ask.

"Mrs. Brown?" I said again.

Mrs. Brown was reading Suzie Knowlton's essay and showed me her palm, which was her way of saying *wait*. Her palm was almost as pale as mine, I do not know why that is with black people, why the two sides of their hands would be such different colors.

I looked at the clock, then looked at Brad Thornton. Brad and his friend Tim Monker were standing right at the door, talking. They were both sort of small, but that didn't stop them from being mean.

"Yes, Nick?" Mrs. Brown asked, standing over me. Mrs. Brown is a very big woman, but when she is not mad, she is not scary at all, even when she stands over you.

"Can a parent stop you from going to college?"

Mrs. Brown just looked at me, and then turned, moved, so her body was between me and the rest of the class. Like I said, Mrs. Brown is pretty large, so when she did that, it was like she was making what we said private. "You want to go to college?"

"Me?" I was embarrassed. That Mrs. Brown would think I would think that. "No, not me. I—I— No!"

"And why not?" Mrs. Brown asked, adjusting one of her bosoms. Mrs. Brown has enormous bosoms, so they need a lot of adjusting.

"Not me. I mean for Hope," I said, in a hurry. "My sister. She wants to go, but how does college work, exactly? Can a parent stop you from going?"

Mrs. Brown didn't say anything. I could see her thinking, though. Mrs. Brown is always thinking, even if she doesn't talk much.

After thinking she looked over her shoulder at the clock on the wall. "We need to talk tomorrow," she said.

And as if she timed it just right, the bell rang.

FOURTEEN

C ollege boy!" Brad shouted, catching up and walking beside me down the hallway toward the science wing. "Nick thinks he can be a college boy."

I just shook my head. Saying anything back to Brad was always a mistake.

"Where are you applying, Nick? Dummy U? Are you going to Dummy U, Nick?"

Tim was right behind us and laughing loud. The hallway was crowded, so no one else was paying attention.

"You better learn your times tables, Nick," Brad said, elbowing me. "Even at Dummy U, you got to know the times tables."

Tim was killing himself laughing, but I kept my eyes straight ahead. I wanted to squash little Brad Thornton, but I didn't do it. And I could tell it was bugging him, that he couldn't get to me.

"Hey Suzie! SUZIE!" Brad saw Suzie Knowlton's blond hair ahead of us. Like I said, every boy in Mrs. Brown's class liked Suzie Knowlton, but Brad was the only one of us who tried to talk to her every chance he got. "Did you hear the latest, Suzie? Nick here thinks he's going to be a college boy."

Suzie looked back at us, biting her lip. For being so pretty, Suzie bit her lip a lot. I am not sure she belonged in Mrs. Brown's class. She always seemed more scared than stupid, like the rest of us.

"Nick thinks he's going to Harvard!"

"I do not," I said, forgetting to shut up.

"He wants you to go, too, Suzie." Brad was leaning his head toward Suzie's hair and talking ugly. "He said he hopes you're in ALL his classes."

"Leave her alone," I said.

Brad leaned even closer behind Suzie. "He wants to be your roommate," he said, talking softer, uglier.

"Leave her alone," I told him.

Brad put his face right in Suzie's hair. "Nick wants you to suck his—"

Brad did not get to say the next word. I should have gotten a teacher, that was what Mrs. Brown would have said, but I knew what word Brad was going to say next and without thinking, I drove my shoulder into him and Brad slammed into the lockers.

I must have hit him pretty hard because when Brad crashed into the lockers, everyone around stopped and looked. Tim bashed his elbow hard into my back, sneaky, so no one could see, but Brad did not do anything. Brad just rubbed his shoulder and looked at me and smiled.

He had won.

He had gotten to me.

And he would get me back later, when it mattered the most.

FIFTEEN

Ms. Lawson, I'm sorry this is taking so long to explain. I wish I could just tell you about the night I found the gun. I hate thinking about that night, hate thinking about holding the gun in my hand, and I just want to get it over with. But you said to tell the whole story, and I think Brad Thornton is part of the story. I wish he wasn't. I wish I hadn't seen him the night I found the gun, but I did. And he saw me. He saw me, and he knew exactly what to do to get me back. He did a good job of getting me back.

SIXTEEN

Work was easier after the first day.

I knew how to tilt the plates in the tray, and Alice showed me how to scrub pots without getting my sleeves all soaked. Alice reminded me of Mrs. Brown. They were both really nice, and I worked as hard as I could to make them happy.

"Hey! Hey! Hey! Easy!"

It was the guy with the pointy mustache. Sam. Sam was the assistant chef, and part of his job was emptying the trays of clean plates and silverware after they came through the dishwasher.

"We're not trying to break any records!" he shouted at me, from the other end of the dishwasher.

I stopped loading the dishwasher and went to work on the pots.

One of the big pots had tomato sauce in it, and when I filled it up from the faucet, the water looked all red and bloody, like I had seen in a movie where there was a battle and people were bleeding into the river. In the movie they played a sad song, showing the river after the battle. Washing the pot, I started whistling that sad song.

Mr. Daniels came by and slapped me on the back. "Good job, Nick."

When Mr. Daniels walked back into his office, Sam walked over.

"Kiss up," he said.

I couldn't tell if Sam was being funny or not, so I just kept my mouth shut. I stopped whistling, though, in case Sam thought that was how I was kissing up.

"Don't mind him," Alice said, bringing over another square tub of dirty dishes and touching my arm. It didn't mean anything, her touching my arm. But it felt nice, just the same.

"Thank you for all your help," I said, feeling my face start to burn.

Alice laughed, loud enough for Sam to turn around and look. "You're quite a blusher," she said.

I looked everywhere but at her.

"It's nice," she said, not laughing anymore.

My heart wouldn't stop beating, after that, even after Alice went back out front and I went back to the bloody looking water.

"You like fat Alice?"

It was Sam. Standing right behind me. He was smiling but didn't look friendly.

"She's not fat," I said.

"Oh, yeah?" Sam squinted and I could tell I was right about his smile, it wasn't friendly at all. He leaned forward. "Ever see her naked? Ever see fat Alice naked?"

I didn't understand. I didn't know what to do.

"I have," Sam said, not smiling at all now. "I've seen her naked a lot. She's my girlfriend, dipshit."

I didn't believe it. I didn't want to, anyway.

Sam smiled again, watching me. Maybe he could tell I didn't believe him. I think he could tell I didn't believe him because he walked over to the doorway and called for Alice. He waved for her to come back, and when she did, when she came through the doorway he put his arm around her.

And kissed her on the lips.

Alice pulled away from him, but not like she was surprised, just embarrassed. When she looked at me, I thought she looked a little sad.

So I knew Sam hadn't lied to me.

Alice really was his girlfriend.

SEVENTEEN

I t turned cold after that.

It was almost Christmas.

Hope and I put up a tree we found behind Walmart. We took the bus there to see if we could afford a tree, and then cutting through the back area by the trucks we found a tree lying there beside a green dumpster.

We took it home and decorated it with the ornaments that did not break three years ago when the tree went through the window and Mom died.

Mrs. Brown had said to tell Hope to talk to her counselor about Dad not wanting her to go to college, so that is what I told Hope.

"Stay out of it," Hope said.

I looked over at Hope. She was behind the tree, hanging the shiny green helicopter. It was one of the ornaments that broke when the tree went through the window, but for some reason, Hope would not throw this one away. Instead she used clear tape to hold it together. The tape was all yellow now, but Hope still always hung the broken helicopter on the back of the tree.

I bit my lip. I had been really wanting to ask Hope this question, but I was so scared of the answer I had to hold my breath. "Are you really going to take me with you?" I said, finally.

Hope did not move, would not look at me. "I wouldn't leave without you," she said, and then reached down into the Christmas box for another ornament.

I felt happy that Hope said she would take me with her, but I felt scared for her, too. What if I made things harder for her? What if she could not really go to college because she felt like she had to take me with her?

"I think I would be OK here," I said.

"*What?*" Hope sounded angry.

Now I was the one who couldn't look at her. "I think I'd be OK," I told her.

"Are you crazy?" Hope asked, but not in a mean way.

"When he drank, I could just stay away," I told her. "I'd be OK."

Hope didn't say anything, and she kept not saying anything, and it got to be so bad I had to look over and see why. She was looking at me, but she wasn't mad. She was smiling. "You're a bad liar, Nick."

EIGHTEEN

At the diner, Alice wasn't as friendly after Sam kissed her in front of me. She wasn't unfriendly—I couldn't picture Alice ever being unfriendly—but when she dropped off the square tubs of dirty dishes, she usually didn't say anything, and she never laughed.

Our eyes met a lot, though. I would wait until she was just about finished unloading her plates out of the tub, and I would go over to start collecting them, and for just a second, our eyes would match up.

I knew it was stupid, but I had never felt anything like it.

Friday that week Alice was wearing a Santa hat but didn't seem very happy. She didn't even joke around with the customers.

Sam was in a great mood, though. He came down to my end of the dishwasher and talked about the great present he got Alice for Christmas.

"You just wait and see!" he said to Alice, as she unloaded dishes. "You're going to love it."

Alice didn't say anything. Didn't meet his eyes. Didn't meet my eyes, either. She just left and went back out front.

Sam looked at me, his cheeriness draining away. "Women don't know shit about us," he said, poking his own chest. "They don't get us at all."

I had no idea what he meant, had no idea what was wrong between the two of them. Not until later, when a dessert plate slipped out of Alice's hand as she was unloading her tray. The plate hit the floor and shattered. Alice bent down to pick up the pieces, and I got down to help.

That was how I saw her thigh. Her skirt had come up on her leg. I was not looking, not really, not that way, but the black blotches were very big. Bruises, dark and ugly. I stopped picking up pieces and just stared.

"Alice," I said.

Alice saw me staring and quickly stood up.

"What is it?" I asked, standing up, too. I thought maybe she was sick, didn't know why someone would bruise like that.

Then Alice's eyes avoided me. And for just a second looked toward the back of the kitchen.

I followed her eyes back and saw Sam.

"I need to get away," she whispered, and disappeared back out front.

NINETEEN

I didn't know who to talk to. Maybe no one. Maybe there was no one to talk to about something like that.

The next day was a good day at school. That can happen sometimes, even when you are stupid. I got a math test back from Mr. Garrison and it was an 82. I was surprised because I didn't really understand negative numbers, but maybe sometimes you understand things better than you think you do. Thanks to Mr. Garrison, maybe negative numbers weren't as hard for me to understand as I thought they were. Mr. Garrison is really good at explaining things in a way even I can understand. Mrs. Adams the year before would sometimes think I was pretending to be stupid, but Mr. Garrison could tell I was not pretending, and he never got mad at me for it.

The 82 felt really good. Especially when I got to Mrs. Brown's class and she made a big deal about it. You would think we were geniuses in that class, if you listened to Mrs. Brown. The only time she ever talked about our grades was when they were good. When I failed tests, Mrs. Brown didn't even seem to see the test papers when I showed them to her. But with the 82 she acted like I was the star of the football team. She was so loud about it, Suzie Knowlton even patted me on the arm and said good job. It was a little embarrassing, but mostly I liked it.

Each of us had a three ring binder just for Mrs. Brown's class, and in our binders were Award Pages, which were made of fancy paper where we were supposed to put the stickers Mrs. Brown gave us every time something good happened. Some teachers put Awards up on the wall, but Mrs. Brown thinks Awards should be private. I don't get many Awards, so I like Mrs. Brown's idea that Awards are private.

For the 82 on the math test Mrs. Brown gave me a whole roll of stickers. She stood there, waiting for me to stick them on my Award Pages, but I really wanted to ask her something, and I was too nervous about it to put the stickers on my Award Pages. I just stuffed the stickers into my three ring binder, hoping Mrs. Brown wouldn't notice, but of course she did.

"What's wrong, Nick?" she asked.

"He got rejected by Harvard," Brad said.

Tim sounded like he was throwing up, he laughed so loud.

"I was wondering," I said, quiet, so Brad could not hear, "when is it OK to hurt someone?"

Mrs. Brown put her big hands flat on my desk and leaned over me. "Is there someone you want to hurt?"

I thought about Sam and what he had done to Alice. "I was just wondering," I lied, shrugging. "It must be OK sometimes to hurt someone."

Mrs. Brown did not move for a long time. "In self-defense," she said, eventually. "If someone wants to hurt you in a serious way, hurting them may be the only way to protect yourself."

"When do you know when that is?" I asked, looking down at her hands on my desk.

"That's a wonderful question, Nick," Mrs. Brown said. "A wonderful question I don't know how to answer, except to say that it should never be fun."

I looked up at Mrs. Brown but didn't understand.

"Never become the bully," she warned me. "Protecting yourself should never be fun."

TWENTY

Ms. Lawson, you may not know why I put that in there. You may not understand why I think Mrs. Brown telling me not to become the bully is part of the story, but I really think it is. I think it's part of the story because when I had the gun in my hand, I *did* become the bully. I didn't realize it that night, but every time I pointed the gun at someone, I was being a bully. And it was fun. It was scary, but it was also fun to point the gun and make people listen. But I was being a bully, an awful bully.

A bully who killed someone.

TWENTY-ONE

The afternoon I talked to Mrs. Brown, my heart was beating hard when I got to work.

"Do you know about self-defense?" I asked Alice, as soon as I saw her. The diner was near the mall, and since it was Christmas, we were busier than usual. Alice was in a hurry, unloading dirty dishes.

"What?" she asked.

"It's OK to self defend," I said.

Alice just shook her head and went back out front. I didn't care, though, I wasn't going to just give up, so I kept an eye out for the next time she came back.

"Do you know karate?" I asked.

"Will you leave me alone?" Her eyes looked past me, back to Sam in the kitchen.

"You need self-defense," I said.

Alice kept her head down. "I don't need self-defense," she said. "I have a gun."

TWENTY-TWO

A gun.

Even the word sounded dangerous. Why would Alice have a gun?

Mom hated guns. It has only been three years since Mom died, but I only have a few clear memories of her. One of them is Mom the morning after Dad brought home a gun. Mom went crazy, stomping, screaming, even breaking plates.

"Guns kill people! Kill people!"

Dad said the neighborhood was not safe, that a lot of blacks had moved in.

"You want to kill the Martins?" Mom asked, pointing to the house across the street. The Martins were a nice old couple. He grew tomatoes. She loved tag sales. "The Kellys? The Smiths?" These were other black families on the street. "Who do you really want to kill? Nick? Hope? Me? Do you want to kill me?"

Dad had been out late the night before. The screaming was hurting him, I could tell. He stood at the kitchen sink, holding on, the meanness right there, freezing his jaw. I thought maybe he *did* want to kill mom. At least right at that moment. At that moment he might have really wanted to kill her.

It made me think having a gun around really was a bad idea. It made me very scared of guns. Sometimes I couldn't get to sleep, thinking about the gun in the cabinet over the refrigerator. That was where Dad kept it. I would lie in bed and think how a bullet can go right into you. It's true, bullets travel so fast they can go right through you. It really scared me, how fast bullets go.

So it scared me when Alice told me she had a gun. The next day at work, I tried talking to her.

"You should get rid of it," I said.

It was even busier than the day before, and Alice was dumping plates without paying attention. "What?" she asked.

"The gun. Why do you have it?"

She looked at me. "Jesus," was all she said, walking away.

But like I said, it was busy, I knew she would need to come back. And when she did, I could tell she was trying to get away before I could say something.

"It's not safe."

"Oh, yeah?" she said, throwing plates down. "You know a lot about safety?"

"Why do you have it?"

Alice tried to laugh. "Maybe I don't know karate."

"Just tell me why."

Alice sighed and stood there, suddenly looking very tired. "In case he goes too far."

TWENTY-THREE

I did a bad thing that night, Ms. Lawson. I started everything that night. It all might have happened, anyway, but I don't think so.

I finished work and went home and ate dinner, like usual. But then I went back to the diner and waited outside.

Alice got off at 8 o'clock. It was windy and I watched her pull the collar of her jacket in tight against the cold.

I knew she lived in the neighborhood because she talked about walking home. I stayed a whole block behind and almost stopped a couple of times.

What was I doing? I still don't know for sure. For some reason I thought if I knew where she lived, maybe she would be safer. I *did* want to protect her. But I also liked her. So maybe I just wanted to know where she lived. I never ever thought I would visit her, so it doesn't make sense that I wanted to know where she lived. But maybe that's part of liking a girl, is that you want to know everything about her. Even if it doesn't make sense.

Alice walked up Freemont to Madison and turned right. The other side of Madison was a bad part of town, even for people who lived where I did.

I ran to the corner and saw Alice a half a block away, under the green shamrocks light of McCann's. McCann's was where Dad went to drink. He said it was one of the only places that didn't have drug dealers. What he meant was it didn't have black people.

Alice crossed the street without barely looking. She was wearing a red hat with a pom-pom that bounced when she leapt off the curb. I imagined putting my arms around her and pulling the hat off by the pom-pom and watching her hair burst out from under the hat.

I knew then for sure I was doing a bad thing. Maybe I wanted to protect Alice, but that wasn't why I was following her like this.

I was following her because I liked her.

I should have stopped right there, but then Alice started climbing stairs to the entrance of this big yellow brick building. She flew up the stairs fast, the pom-pom bouncing, and disappeared inside. I felt sad, seeing her disappear. I kept walking until I was standing in front of the entrance, looking at the lighted doorway.

This was where Alice lived. It felt important, like a church, and I stood there a moment, just breathing.

"Hey, it's Nick College!"

My stomach did a twisty thing. Over to the left, sticking his head out a second story window, was Brad Thornton from Mrs. Brown's class. I knew he lived across the street from McCann's, but I didn't know he lived in this building.

"How are those college applications going, Nicky?"

I decided not to care. He could holler what he wanted from up there. I stuck my hands in my pockets and turned my back on him and started to leave.

That was when he said it.

"Walking your girlfriend home?" Brad hollered. And then, because I walked faster, he hollered louder. "Sam told me you worked together!"

He knew Sam! Brad knew Sam. I started to run.

"Sam's not going to like it, you walking fat Alice home!" Brad yelled after me.

TWENTY-FOUR

I felt sick. Walking home, making my lunch for the next day, trying to get to sleep, all I could think about was Brad telling Sam. He would do it, I knew he would do it.

He would tell Sam that I had followed Alice home.

TWENTY-FIVE

I didn't want to go to school the next day. When you are as stupid as me, you never want to go to school, but that morning was worse than all the other mornings combined.

I just wanted to stay under the covers and go back to sleep.

"Hey! Hey!" Hope said, poking at the covers. "You sick?"

I thought about this. "Yeah," I said.

"Get up, faker," Hope said, poking harder but not mean. "Are you working today?"

"I guess so." Going to work would be even worse than going to school.

"Stop by here on the way to work and get the mail, OK? I've been getting it every day, but today I'm working late. So you need to get it. Don't forget."

"What's the big deal?"

Hope lowered her voice. "I should be hearing

from that college any day now," she said. "I don't want Dad burning the letter and claiming it never came."

Hearing about the letter scared me. "What if he finds out?" I asked.

"He won't find out," Hope said.

"He has to find out," I said, sitting up in bed. "What is he going to do to you?"

"He doesn't scare me."

"He should," I said. And that was when I thought about the cabinet above the refrigerator. I thought about the cabinet above the refrigerator, and I thought about protecting Hope.

"Just worry about the letter," Hope said. "I can take care of myself."

TWENTY-SIX

I was able to avoid Brad Thornton all the way to seventh period, but he was there in Mrs. Brown's class. When I walked in, he saw me and elbowed Tim.

"Lover boy," Brad said, and pursed his lips, making kissing sounds. "Likes 'em fat, Nick does. Fat and juicy, huh, Nicky? Big sloppy peaches, huh, Nicky?" He made disgusting sounds with his tongue and lips, and Mrs. Brown walked over and stood in front of him.

"Do you need to see the nurse, Mr. Thornton?"

Other people in the class laughed. Even Suzie Knowlton, who is very pretty but doesn't laugh much. Even Suzie laughed.

Brad leaned over to look past Mrs. Brown at me. I wasn't laughing, but he looked at me angry, like I was. He looked at me like it was my fault Suzie Knowlton was laughing at him.

"I told everyone about your girlfriend," he said, a smile pushing through the anger. "*Everyone.*"

It wasn't until later that night that I found out what he meant. But looking across at Brad there in the classroom, I knew one thing for sure.

I knew Brad wanted to hurt me in a serious way.

TWENTY-SEVEN

Alice wasn't at work when I got there. Christmas was only two days away, so it was crazy busy.

"You see Alice?" Mr. Daniels asked, as I put on my apron. He was mad and snapped his fingers, wanting me to answer fast.

"N-N-N-No."

I saw Mr. Daniels go back and ask Sam something, but Sam just shrugged and shook his head. He shook his head and then turned and looked at me. He looked at me hard, and I tried to look away without seeming guilty or scared. But he knew, he knew about me following Alice home, I could tell. There was no doubt he knew, no doubt Brad had told him.

I worked on the pots and after awhile Alice came in, wearing a baseball cap real low, hiding her eyes. I was very glad she was finally there, but she walked right by without saying hello or even waving.

I wanted to say I was sorry, but I didn't know how, so I didn't say anything. I just felt bad every time Alice dropped off a square tub of dirty dishes and used the baseball cap to keep her eyes away from me.

This went on for a long time. It might have gone on until I left if I hadn't dropped one of the big spaghetti pots. It was slippery from the soap, and it went right out of my hands and crashed down on the brick-colored tile. Clang! It was so loud, I jumped. Alice was emptying another tub of dishes and looked up at the sound.

And I saw her eye.

"Oh, God."

It was red and purple and thick and almost closed.

I saw it. I saw it and Alice saw me seeing it. And I couldn't say anything, nothing would come out of my mouth.

And Alice was gone.

I couldn't think for a long time after that, just couldn't think at all, kept running hot water into the big pots. I ran water and held onto the edge of the sink.

It was my fault. Brad Thornton told Sam I followed Alice, and Sam beat Alice up bad. Because of what I did. It was all my fault

When Alice came back, I went right over, I didn't care if she didn't want me to, I didn't care who saw me talking to her.

"You need to get out," I said. "You need to get away."

Alice dropped her head so her whole face was hidden by the baseball cap. She dropped her head and stood there very still, like she was praying. I wouldn't have had any idea what was going on but I saw a tear land on her blue shirt sleeve. First one tear, and then another. I didn't know what to do.

"You need to get away tonight," I said. "Tonight, Alice." She didn't move. I didn't know if she could even hear me. "Alice?"

"Help me," she said.

TWENTY-EIGHT

I couldn't stop washing pots after that. I washed pots, I filled trays with dishes, I even cleaned the whole sink. And when I got off work, I ran home.

Alice got off work at 9 o'clock. And Sam didn't get off work until 10. That meant we had an hour. One hour to get Alice out of their apartment. I was scared for so many reasons, my mind kept spinning around and around.

I was scared Alice would change her mind and would decide to stay.

I was scared we wouldn't know how to carry all her stuff.

And I was scared she would have no place to go. What would we do then? On the day before Christmas Eve, where could we go?

I was scared but I was also excited that I could help her. If I could get her away from Sam, I would really be helping her.

It wasn't until I got all the way home and came through the door and heard the television on loud that I remembered.

The mail!

I had forgotten all about getting the mail.

Hope had counted on me, and I had completely forgotten.

"*Hope*?" Dad called, his voice sounding like rock.

"No," I called back, feeling sick for being so stupid. Stupid, stupid, stupid.

There were no lights on in the entire house except the television. I hung my jacket on the hook by the door and walked over and turned on the light over the stove. There were so many beer cans in the sink I couldn't even count them.

Which meant the letter had come. The letter from the college. The letter I promised Hope I would get before Dad did.

Dad had gotten the letter out of the mailbox.

And he knew the college had said yes to Hope.

If they had told Hope no, Dad still would have been drunk, but he would have had all the lights on. He would have been happy in a mean way.

Now he was unhappy in a mean way. Which was way worse.

I needed to do something. This was my fault. And I needed to do something.

I needed to be the one Dad took it out on.

Hope had done that for me lots of times, had seen Dad getting mad at me and had done something to really annoy him so he would be mad at her instead.

And I knew just what would get Dad really angry. Light. When he was sitting in the dark watching television, he would go crazy if you started turning on lights that would spill into the living room.

I turned on the overhead light in the kitchen and waited.

Nothing.

I went into the bathroom and turned on that light.

Nothing.

The hallway was right outside the living room, and I held my breath, turning on that light.

Still nothing.

From the hallway I could see the back of Dad's head. For a second I thought maybe he was asleep, but then he took a drink from the beer can in his hand.

I looked over at the dark Christmas tree.

When Dad was drinking, he hated the lights of the Christmas tree more than anything. One time he came home and not only unplugged the lights, he used a knife to cut off the plug. Hope had to go out and buy more lights.

I swallowed down my fear and walked into the living room and reached down and plugged in the lights on the Christmas tree.

Instead of screaming, Dad hit the mute button on the remote. I stepped back, it got so quiet.

"Real brave now that you think you have a girl-friend, huh?"

TWENTY-NINE

I couldn't move.

"I was at McCann's last night," Dad said, not turning around to face me. "Your friend Brad told me all about you and the fat girl."

Now I knew why Brad had smiled in Mrs. Brown's class. I knew why he had said he had told *everyone*. He hadn't just told Sam. He told my dad, too.

"She's not your girlfriend, you know," Dad said.

All I could do was stand there.

"Following a girl home does not make her your girlfriend, do you know that?"

I needed to get away. Dad was just going to get meaner and meaner, and I almost walked away. But then in the Christmas lights I saw the letter. The letter from the college, the letter for Hope, the letter Dad got out of the mailbox that day.

It was unfolded on Dad's metal tray. At the top of the page I could read *College* in fancy lettering.

When I saw the letter, I knew I needed to stand there. Even Dad had only so much meanness. If I could wear the meanness down, maybe it wouldn't be so bad for Hope when she got home.

"Are you too stupid to realize that fat girl will never be your girlfriend?"

I did not move.

"Are you too stupid to realize she would never want you?"

I stuffed my hands in my pockets and squeezed my fists.

Dad sat up and turned around to face me. "Hey, Thick. Are you really that stupid? Don't you see she's just using you, Thick? Don't you see that? Are you really that thick? That you can't see how she's just using you to make her fella jealous?"

I knew it was just Dad trying to be mean, but with Dad it was hard not to listen to the words, hard not to think he was right.

"You are so stupid, Thick," he said, shaking his head. "Do you even know what a girlfriend is? Do you know what a girlfriend does?"

I could feel my face, my whole head burning.

"A girlfriend kisses you," Dad said. "Did you know that? A girlfriend wants to kiss you."

I wanted to go outside and feel the coldness.

"Do you think any girl would ever want to kiss you?" Dad squinted at me. "Do you, Thick? Do you think any girl would ever want to f--- you?"

I turned away and headed out of the living room, but Dad got up and followed me, spitting the words at my back.

"Do you think a girl would ever want to touch your c---?"

I kept walking

"Do you think a girl would ever let you touch her c---?"

I hated that word. Hated it. I walked into the bathroom and tried to close the door, but Dad blocked the door with his foot.

"What's the matter, little boy?" Dad was smiling now. "You don't like hearing the word c---? Every woman has one, you know. Every woman has a c---."

He sounded angry, like he was mad that I didn't like that word, didn't want to hear it.

"Maybe you're a c---, Thick. Are you a c---?"

I pushed by him into the kitchen. Headed straight for the door. Dad followed me. He knew I was leaving and started talking faster.

"No girl is ever going to want to f--- you, Thick," Dad said, following me into the kitchen. "They'd never f--- you because they'd be too terrified that they'd end up with a baby. A baby that was just as thick a mother-f----- as you are."

I grabbed my jacket while Dad kept yelling at me, saying the worst words he could say, calling me the worst things. I quick yanked the door open.

And saw Hope there with her keys out, her eyes wide.

THIRTY

But Dad was too angry and drunk to care what words Hope may have heard through the door. He just stopped for a second, looking at her.

"Well, if it isn't the little college c---!"

It was like he hit Hope. "Dad!" I said.

"Shut up."

But I wasn't going to shut up. I would never shut up. "Dad, don't. Don't!"

He pushed me aside and started growling at Hope. He used the word again.

"Stop it!" I shouted, pulling hard at his shoulder. Dad swung his arm, pushing me down.

"Leave him out of this!" Hope shouted.

"Just go!" I told her. "Get away!"

"That's right, go!" Dad shouted. "Go away, college c---!"

Something went off inside me. That was it, that was it, I wasn't going to let Hope hear that word again.

I got to my knees and dove at Dad. I hit him from the side, hard, and his legs went out from under him. He fell, toppled over on top of me.

I didn't know what else to do. I had no idea what else to do and just held onto his legs.

"What the— You little—" Dad sounded even madder, huffing and puffing. Like a big animal breaking its chains, he kicked his legs free, one heel colliding with my mouth. The pain wasn't as bad as the sickening taste of blood, warm and salty. But then Dad kicked again, his boot smashing into my nose. Tears came to my eyes, the pain was so bad.

"Get off him, get off him!" Hope screamed, somewhere overhead.

Dad was cursing and punching and grabbing at me, and I could hear Hope screaming and punching, too. And then Dad wrapped his arm around my face and yanked my head back.

"Get off me or I'll kill him," Dad shouted. "I'll kill him, goddammit!"

I was belly down on the floor. Dad had something hard, a knee maybe, in my back, and he had a hold of my head and was bending it back, way back, back so far I was groaning in pain.

"You're crazy!" Hope screamed at him. "Crazy! Crazy! Crazy!"

I never heard her sound so scared.

"Get out of my house, get out of my goddam house or he's dead. I'll kill him, I swear I'll f---ing kill him."

Hope looked down at me, her face squeezed with pain. "Nick! Oh, Jesus, Nick!"

I could hardly talk, Dad had my head pulled so far back. "Please, Hope," I cried, blood thick in my mouth.

"Get out of my sight, get out of my f---ing sight and you'll still have a brother!"

Hope grabbed her hair with both hands, her eyes shut tight.

"Please!" I pleaded, tears filling my eyes, blinding me. I couldn't see what was happening, but I heard the door slam.

And Dad let go of me.

I was crying. I didn't want to, but my neck and my nose hurt so bad I couldn't help it. I blinked the tears out of my eyes. I was still belly down on the floor and could see a string of snotty blood dripping down.

Dad was huffing and puffing as he stood up. "I'll kill her," he said, his voice low and mean. "I'm going to kill her."

I didn't know if he meant it. Maybe he did, maybe he didn't, I didn't know for sure. But I knew how to stop him. I pushed myself up to my knees and crawled and then stood up, my legs wobbly, and stumbled into the kitchen. Hope had some books piled up on top of the refrigerator, and I quick knocked them off and heard them crash to the floor as I opened the cabinet.

Which was empty. I opened both doors, but the cabinet was completely empty.

"You dumb little shit," Dad said, laughing as he stood in the doorway.

"Where is it?" I asked.

He kept laughing. "Your mother took it, you dumb little shit."

"You're lying," I said.

"You still think she got hit by a car, don't you? You don't even know that your mother blew her own f--- ing brains out."

"You're lying," I said again, even though I knew he wasn't. I could tell by the coldness in his voice that he wasn't lying.

"She was weak," he said. "Your mother was weak and stupid."

"Liar."

"That's where you get it from, Thick. That's—" He stopped and turned his head.

That was when I heard it, too—sirens. Sirens, close and getting closer.

"*Shit!*" Dad turned and rushed over and grabbed his jacket off the peg. He pulled open the door and then looked back at me and pointed. "Tell your sister if she comes back to my house, I'll kill her."

Like he killed Mom, I thought, as he slammed the door closed behind him. I wasn't confused. I understood what Dad had said. I knew Mom had killed herself.

But that didn't mean Dad didn't kill her with his meanness.

He had. He had killed her. With his meanness to her and his meanness to us, I knew he'd pushed Mom to do it. And I could feel something cold filling my chest, knowing that Dad was the reason Mom was dead.

The sirens sounded very close now, and I realized I couldn't stay, either. The police would want to talk to me. They would ask me questions. They would find out about the cold hate in my chest.

I stood up, wiping blood off my mouth and chin, my nose still making me cry.

I grabbed my jacket and was gone.

THIRTY-ONE

The police car was already loud on our street when I got outside.

I cut across our small backyard, my legs shaky, my head dizzy. It was dark and I tripped over weeds where Mom's garden had been.

The siren was screaming now, the police car stopping out front, red lights swinging by, and I jumped for the fence to the train tracks, leapt over the fence like I was a criminal they were going to catch. I couldn't hold onto to the top like I was supposed to, though, and I landed on the little steep hill and started sliding fast.

Started sliding fast toward the top of the wall, the wall with the train tracks down below.

A train was roaring past down there racing toward New York City.

I clutched and clawed at anything, trying to slow down, but there was nothing but trash that had been blown there for years.

I hit the top of the wall on my side, still rolling, sliding, my body going over the wall but my fingers grabbing hold of the outside edge.

Wrappers, cans, bottles kept going, right past me, falling, the bottles smashing on top of the train. I pulled myself back up to the top of the wall and laid there, breathing through my mouth, my nose dripping something warm.

I was very glad to be alive.

Very glad I was still there to stop things from happening ever again.

THIRTY-TWO

I do not know if I wanted to kill my father, Ms. Lawson. You asked when you came here if I ever wanted to kill my father, and I might have, lying there on the wall in the dark, everything getting quiet after the train had gone by.

I know I wanted to stop him. I don't remember having a plan or knowing what to do. But I know I wanted to stop him from ever doing to Hope what he did to Mom.

I didn't care what I had to do, either, I know that. I know if I had to kill him to stop him from hurting Hope, I'd do it. I'd do anything to make sure Hope got away.

But as soon as thought that, I thought of Alice. I'd forgotten Alice. And that night, she needed my help more than anybody. I had to go help Alice.

THIRTY-THREE

It was after nine by the time I got to Madison Avenue.

My lip was big and split, and my nose was clogged with blood and it hurt even without touching it, but the cold had stopped the bleeding.

I ran up the steps outside Alice's building and tried the door, but it was locked. I looked at the black buttons on the side. *Hillman.* Alice's last name was Hillman, but I couldn't find it

What was Sam's last name? I couldn't remember, and I had no idea what to do. I stood there, breathing through my mouth, and could see my breath from the cold.

And then things got worse because through the glass in the door I could see Brad inside. Brad Thornton was walking toward the door, zipping up his jacket.

Had he seen me from his window? Had he come down to start a fight? I was scared to fight with my

nose already hurting the way it did, but I took my
hands out of my pockets as Brad opened the door. If I
had to fight him, I would.

But instead of fighting, Brad flung the door open
and walked right by me.

"Nice face," was all he said.

I did not pay attention. I just grabbed the door
before it closed.

"Three-C, lover boy," Brad called, not looking back.

I watched the back of his head as he hopped
down the stairs. He was lying. I held onto the door
and knew he had to be lying.

But maybe the people in 3-C would know where
Alice lived.

I ran up the steps, my nose pounding to my
heartbeat. Three-C was right at the stairs. I was having a hard time breathing, partly from the clump of
snot and blood in my nose, and partly from being so
out-of-breath scared.

I knocked. And waited.

"Who is it?"

"Alice?" I couldn't believe it. Brad didn't lie to me.
This was the right apartment.

Locks unlocked. The door opened. And there was
Alice. Her eye make-up was smeared black, but it was
Alice, looking worried and then seeing me and step-
ping back.

"Oh, my God."

THIRTY-FOUR

Alice pointed at my face. "Sam. Sam did this."

I shook my head and put my hand in front of my nose, not wanting Alice to look at it.

"Nick, don't lie."

"It was my Dad," I told her.

Alice seemed not ready to believe this. "What happened?"

I stepped inside and closed the door. Closed the door but did not lock it.

"Nick, tell me what happened," Alice said, holding onto my arm with both hands.

But I shook my head. "What do you want to take? We need to get out of here."

"I can't," Alice said, still looking at my face. My face was scaring her. "I can't go. I'm sorry. You need to leave, Nick."

I pointed at my nose. "Sam didn't do this!" I told her, and then pointed at her eye. "But he did that!"

"He'll be nice," Alice said, shaking her head. "He's always nice afterwards. It'll be OK."

"Why? Why did he do it?"

Alice shook her head.

"Just tell me why he did it. Was it me?"

But Alice wouldn't look at me. She kept shaking her head. "You need to go."

"He found out I followed you home," I said. "He beat you up because I followed you home."

"Just leave. Please, Nick. Just leave."

"He's going to know, Alice. He's going to know I'm here."

Alice shook her head hard. "He won't know. Just leave now, he'll never know."

"Brad saw me!" I shouted. "Downstairs! He just saw me."

Alice looked at me terrified. Looked at me like I was going to beat her. "Brad saw you?"

That was when I realized. Of course! Of course that was why Brad didn't lie. That was why Brad told me the real apartment number.

He wanted me here. He wanted me here for when he told Sam. He was probably right that second running over to the diner.

Alice kept staring. "Brad saw you?"

Something fell against the other side of the door.

Alice screamed.

THIRTY-FIVE

"**R**un! Run!" she said, pulling at me, then pushing at me down a short hallway and into a room. A small room that was the living room and kitchen, a couch by the window, a sink, stove, and refrigerator in the corner. "There's a fire escape!" Alice shouted. "Run!"

A laugh came at us as the door burst open. "Don't worry, little girl, he'll run."

Both Alice and I stopped and stared. Alice because she did not know who this man was. And me because I did.

"Right, son?" Dad said, laughing again. "You'll run. Go ahead, run, son! Run!"

Alice looked at me.

"Dad, get out of here," I said. But my voice was shaky, saying it. My voice gave me away.

"Your father?" Alice asked, confused.

"Go away," I told him.

Dad laughed and closed the door behind him and locked it.

"Get out," I said.

"Scared, wussy boy?" Dad lost his balance and reached out for the wall "My little boy. The p-----."

"Why is he here?" Alice asked, pushing past me and looking at Dad. "What are you doing here?"

"Someone came into McCann's and told me where my son was," Dad said, walking past Alice toward me. "I'm here to tell Thick here to keep his nose out of other people's business."

"You need to leave," Alice told him. "You need to leave now."

Dad gave me a shove, pushed me down the little hallway and back into the small room. "My son's stupid." He tried to push me again but I wouldn't let him.

"*You're* stupid," I said.

Dad laughed, looking at me, and talked louder. "My stupid son thinks you want him, little lady."

"I never said that."

"He's stupid enough to think you want to f--- him."

"Stop it," I warned him.

"You need to leave," Alice said, grabbing Dad's arm from behind.

Dad just stood there swaying, looking at me. "Think you're going to get some? Think you're going to get a piece of ass?"

Alice moved around and stepped in front of him. "I want you to leave."

Dad kept smiling, looking from me to Alice. He walked forward into her, moving his body against her. "You sure, honey? Sure you don't want a real man?"

I pulled Alice away. "Get out of here," I told Dad, my voice different now, my mouth set.

Dad's smile disappeared. He looked at me, his mouth small, and then his arm shot out and shoved me back further into a room.

"Leave him alone," Alice said, seeing Dad stepping toward me.

"You are so goddam stupid," Dad said, sneering, pushing his face toward mine, "women have to protect you."

I put my hands on my hips, staring back at him. "Not anymore," I told him.

Dad smiled slowly. Then quick, before I was ready, he shoved me with both hands, sending me flying back onto couch. "Sit down, tough guy."

I reached down to push myself off the couch and felt something hard, between the cushions. Something hard and cold. I grabbed it in my fist before realizing what it was.

Her gun.

THIRTY-SIX

My hand slipped so easily around the handle, my finger on the trigger. The gun was smooth and clean and felt like it fit me just right, like it was the perfect size for my hand.

"Nick, no," Alice said.

I looked at her.

"Leave it," she said.

I wondered how she knew. How did she know I'd found the gun? Did she see something on my face? Did I look different? Bigger? Stronger? Happier? I felt all those things, and I wondered if Alice saw them.

"Don't," she said.

Dad laughed at her. "What do you think he's going to do? He's not going to do shit, little lady. He going to sit there and hope you protect him."

"You killed Mom," I said, my hand holding on tight to the gun.

Dad squinted at me. "Your mother killed herself. I had nothing to do with it."

"You killed her," I said, feeling meanness I did not know I had inside me.

"You dumb shit!" Dad shouted, ready to attack, ready to grab hold of me and start swinging. I squeezed the gun, waiting for him, ready for him. "She killed herself! Are you too stupid to understand what that means? Your mother took my gun and got a room in a sleazy motel full of whores and drug dealers, and she sat on the filthy bed in that room and blew her f---ing brains out!"

"Because of you."

Dad squeezed his hands into fists. "You dumb shit!" he said, taking a step toward me.

Alice saw me moving my hand. "Nick, no," she said.

A pounding burst at us from the door. "Alice, unlock the door! *Now!*"

THIRTY-SEVEN

Alice stood frozen, her mouth open. She looked ready to cry.

"Alice, I'm warning you!" Sam screamed through the door. "I'm warning you, goddamit!"

Dad was still laughing and pointed at me. "He's going to kick your ass, boy. He's going to kick the living shit out of you."

"Nick." Alice sat down next to me and spoke quiet so Dad could not hear. "I need the gun. Please."

The door was only wood. I didn't think it would hold.

"Open this goddam door!" Sam shouted

Dad smiled, swinging his thumb toward the door. "You better let him in."

"Nick, Sam is *my* problem," Alice said, starting to cry and then fighting it away. She wiped an eye and breathed hard. "Just give me the gun, Nick."

"Shit," Dad said, having fun, turning and lurching toward the hallway, "if you won't let him in, I will."

"Stop!" I shouted. And when he wouldn't, I pulled the gun out and stood up and pointed it at him. "STOP!"

Dad must have heard something in the way I said it because he looked back. The gun made the fun go out of his face. He lost his balance and grabbed the wall.

I held the gun with two hands, pointed at my father.

"Give me the gun," Alice said, standing up beside me. "Just give me the gun, Nick."

Dad watched me, scared. He'd never looked at me like that.

"Give her the gun," he said. He tried to sound like he wasn't scared, but now he was the one with the shaky voice. Now he was the one whose voice was giving himself away.

And my whole body felt alive and powerful because now Dad was scared of me.

THIRTY-EIGHT

"**N**ick, please," Alice said. "You don't even have the safety on."

"You're not opening that door," I told Dad.

"Don't be so f---ing stupid."

"You're not going to open the door," I told him again. "Do you understand?"

But Dad wouldn't understand. He wouldn't listen. If he had just said all right, if he had just promised to not open the door. If he had just tried to understand. I had a gun in my hand. Why didn't he try to understand?

The pounding on the door didn't stop. "Goddammit, Alice, you're going to pay for this! You're going to pay!"

Alice reached out. "Nick, just let me put the safety on."

"No," I said. I didn't trust her, didn't trust anyone. I wasn't going to let anyone take that gun away from me. Alice reached again for the gun. "No!" I said again, pulling it from her.

Dad shied away, like a scared dog. "Nick!"

I shook the gun at him, still holding it with both hands. I could feel blood coming out of my nose but did not dare wipe it.

"Jesus, Nick," Alice said, "give me the gun."

I just shook my head. Alice sounded really scared now, and I didn't think she would keep the gun pointed at anyone.

Sam was kicking hard, but the wooden door still held. "It's my goddam apartment! Open the door! Now!"

"We need to open the door," Dad said, "or someone's going to call the police."

"You're not opening the door," I told Dad.

Dad pointed at Alice. "Then let her open it."

"No one is opening the door," I said. I was getting a little scared now. Things were going very fast, and I couldn't think, and the gun was feeling heavy in my hands. I could see no way out. I didn't see how to stop this, didn't know what to do.

"I'm opening the door," Dad said.

"No, you're not."

Dad took a slow step back. "I'm going to open it."

"No," I said, moving, too.

Dad was near the door now and stopped and just looked at me. Looked at me like he usually did. Like I was disgusting to look at. "You are so f---ing stupid."

I pulled the trigger.

THIRTY-NINE

I pointed the gun up at the ceiling and pulled the trigger. The gun almost fell out of my hands. Between the sound and the way the gun kicked at me, I almost dropped it.

Alice screamed. "*Nick!*"

The pounding on the door stopped.

It was very quiet. Plaster fell from the ceiling, and far away a dog was barking, but the anger in the gunshot stopped everything else.

I felt like the guy in Greek times who Mrs. Brown told us about. The guy who stood on the clouds with a thunderbolt in his hand.

Now I had the thunderbolt.

And my dad had his hands in front of him, trying to protect himself. He was scared, very scared, and when I pointed the gun back at his head, he stepped away and said nothing. Nothing, nothing, nothing!

For a minute I actually felt happy.

"Oh, Jesus Christ, Nick." Alice was beginning to cry.

"It's OK," I told her. I didn't take my eyes off of my father, kept the gun pointed straight at his head. "Alice, it's OK. My father is not going to open the door. He's not going to let Sam in. He's not going to use bad words in front of my sister. And he's not going to stop her from going to college."

My father kept his hands in front of him, his wrists crossed over his chest.

"My father is going to leave us alone. All of us alone."

"Alice?" It was Sam, calling from the other side of the door. He didn't sound angry anymore. "Alice, are you OK?"

"They are all going to leave us alone from now on."

My lungs were full of air. Alice was crying, her hands covering her face, but I knew what to do. I felt smart. I knew what to do and people were going to listen to me.

I kept the gun pointed at my father as I walked slowly around him. I was headed to the door. I was going to tell Sam to leave, leave and never come back. And then I was going to open the door and my father was going to leave, leave and never come back.

And everyone would be safe.

FORTY

I walked around Dad toward the door, still pointing the gun at him, at his face.

Alice's voice shook. "God, Nick, please, please."

"It's OK," I told her, not wanting to hear her cry, hating how she sounded like I was hurting her. "It's going to be OK."

Alice sniffled. "No! No, it's not. It's not going to be OK."

"Alice," I said, but I didn't know what to say, didn't know how to calm her down. She didn't seem to understand that the gun was power, the gun would keep us safe.

"Give her the gun," Dad whispered through his fear, "and no one will be hurt."

But I knew that was a lie. It was a lie that no one would be hurt. He would hurt us, I knew if I gave up the gun, my father would hurt us.

I had to keep the gun, I had no choice. The gun meant everything—whoever had the gun had everything.

And nothing bad would happen as long as I was the one who had the gun.

I knew this was true. I walked toward the door, knowing if I had the gun, people would listen and everything would be OK.

"Give me the gun, Nick."

It was Dad. It was my father, walking toward me.

"Stay back," I told him. I knew how Dad worked, I knew he would move slow, and move slow, and then suddenly do something I wasn't expecting. He would try to push me, or kick me, or try to knock the gun out of my hand.

"We can call the police," Alice said. "Nick, we can call the police."

"They won't do anything," I said.

"We can make them do something," Alice said. "We'll make them, Nick."

Dad was still walking slowly toward me.

"Stop," I told him, my arms feeling tired. The gun was heavy, maybe Dad could tell that the gun was heavy.

"Nick, let me call the police right now, and you can give THEM the gun," Alice said.

"They won't use it," I said, feeling my arms getting strong again, pointing the gun right between Dad's two eyes. "I'll use it," I told him. I didn't think he believed me, but I could feel the anger filling me up. I knew it was true.

I was standing at the door, right at the door, ready to use the gun, ready if Dad tried to do something. My arms were tight with holding the gun, and I wasn't ready for Sam pounding on the door right at that moment, cracking the top of the door with something hard and heavy.

I jumped, sure Sam had a weapon, something dangerous.

I pointed the gun at the door, the gun moving everywhere.

"I'll shoot!" I yelled, fear, real fear in my voice, Sam pounding, the door splintering more, and Dad swung around, Dad was on me, grabbing me, cursing me, Sam reaching through the cracked open door.

"No!" Alice screamed.

Dad had a hold of my hand, had a hold of the gun, and I ground my teeth, twisting, using all my strength, using my whole self to turn the gun and pull the trigger, I pulled and the gun exploded in my ears and there was blood everywhere.

FORTY-ONE

And Alice was dying.

FORTY-TWO

Blood. I know Dad was yelling, I know Sam was pounding on the door, but all I could think about was the blood. So much blood, so red, so fast.

Alice grabbed at me, her face surprised. She looked surprised.

"Alice. Alice!" I dropped the gun and reached for her, my eyes filling with tears, burning. "Alice!"

She couldn't speak, her mouth open but no words, and then blood, blood on her lips as she let go of me, her weight suddenly heavy. I held on, cradling her down to the floor, her eyes opened wide, but her neck loose, her head falling back.

"God, God, God," I cried, my father hitting me, kicking me, Sam pushing through the door and screaming.

"You killed her! You killed her!"

Alice's eyes still wide open, unseeing.

FORTY-THREE

That was what happened, Ms. Lawson.

I shot Alice dead. The bullet went straight through her heart. The doctors tore her open and found out. I was trying to protect Alice, trying to save her, and I shot a bullet right through her heart.

Hope wants me to say that the gun went off because Dad was pulling it out of my hand, but that is not true. I still had the gun, and I was never going to let him get it.

Hope also wants me to say it was an accident, the gun going off, but it was not an accident. I pulled the trigger. It was a decision. I decided to pull the trigger because I was never going to let my father have the gun. I didn't mean to hurt Alice, I never meant to hurt Alice, but I still pulled the trigger.

Dad was still punching and kicking me when the police came, and he got arrested, too, but he is out now and no one knows where. He didn't go back to his job. Hope is living with Mrs. Brown now. Mrs. Brown drives Hope over here to visit. She says Hope can stay with her until she graduates from high school.

And then Hope is going to go to college. Just like she said she would all along.

They will sometimes give us the leftover newspaper in here, and so I was able to read about Alice's funeral. They don't know where her father is, but her mother was at the funeral. She thinks I should get the electric chair for what I did. It hurt, reading that, but I don't blame her at all. Alice was such a nice person, it only seems fair.

Sometimes I can close my eyes and picture Alice's mother shooting me dead. It is not a bad thing to think about, it really is not. Sometimes it helps to think about that when I am trying to get to sleep. I think about Alice's mother shooting me dead, and I can get to sleep OK.

I do deserve to go to prison. It is a bad, bad thing I did, and prison will make me remember, every day, the bad thing I did. I am very scared, though. Please don't tell Hope but I cry sometimes, I am so scared. I think anybody would be scared of prison, but being in here with these men has made me understand that prison is even worse than people think.

It will only be about four years, though. Hope cried when I told her you said that, Ms. Lawson, when you were here, that you thought they would send me to prison for about four years. Maybe it will be longer, now that I wrote this and told the truth, but I hope you are right, I hope it is four years. Hope thinks that four years is a long time, but I think she forgets what I did. I think four years isn't very long when I think about what I did. I pulled a trigger on purpose and a very nice person died. I think most people would think four years was not long enough when they think about what I did.

I am very scared about those four years, but four years is how long Hope will be in college, and maybe then we can live together after that, at least until she gets married and has children. I asked Hope if we could live together when she finished college and I finished prison, and that was when she really cried.

"I just hope it doesn't change you, Nick."

That is Hope's biggest fear, that prison will change me. And maybe it will, but I don't think so, and this is why.

I don't think prison will change me because I think Mom was right, what she said about being stupid. Only mean people are stupid. I think I believe that. Having that gun in my hand gave me a way to be mean. And it gave me a way to be stupid.

What is strange is that I didn't *feel* stupid. The gun made me feel the opposite. I felt really smart with that gun. People were going to listen to me, and that made me feel very smart.

When really I was being the stupidest I have ever been.

This is something that I know now. Being mean is a lot worse than being dumb.

So I'm very very scared of prison, but I'm not scared that prison will change me. I'm not scared that prison will make me ever want to buy a gun. I'm not scared that prison will make me want to be mean.

I am not that stupid any more.

Colin Neenan has been a chauffeur, a waiter, a landscaper, a busboy and a doorman. Now a high school librarian in Connecticut, he has a hard time finding books for kids who hate to read, and he wanted to write one that almost any high school kid could read and enjoy. He's also a runner, a hiker, a reader, an arguer, and the father of two girls. THICK is his fourth book.

IDIOT!

by Colin Neenan

ISBN: 0974648116, $8.95

"Stop, stop, stop, stop, STOP," Mr. Fricker called, walking down the center aisle through the dark of the auditorium. "Look—." He glanced down at his clipboard, then looked up at me. "Jim. Let me ask you. Have you ever been in love?"

I was standing at the edge of the stage, Mr. Fricker down below. I could have easily swung my leg and kicked him in the face.

"Have you ever been in love?"

I was nervous as hell, as it was, standing there center stage, under the only lights in the entire auditorium, saying these words I didn't understand, having a hard time even reading them because my right hand holding the little book was shaking. Why was he doing this?

Mr. Fricker looked back at his clipboard. "Have you ever been in love, Jim?" he asked, in his contemptuous hyper mode. He'd gone insane like this in class, too, whenever someone read a famous poem out loud and stumbled over words and completely butchered it. It was like Fricker took it personally.

"Have you?" he asked, when I didn't answer right away. "Have you ever been in love?"

What the hell was I supposed to say? No? Was I supposed to say no? Was it so obvious? The entire auditorium was completely quite. Fifty or so kids sitting out in the auditorium, all of them watching me hanging there in the wind. Jodi Woodrow. Lisa Kellerman. Bart Fulton. Exchanging looks, smiles. They loved Mr. Fricker. Loved how he could do this to people.

"It's a simple yes or no question," he said, his hands bubbling up in the air like he was re-enacting a volcano. "Have you ever been in love? Have you ever connected to one person in a way that was completely different from how you felt about anyone else in the entire world?"

I don't know why, but my eyes suddenly glanced at Zanny, and my heart flopped like a fish in the bottom of a row boat.

"Yes," I whispered, looking away quickly.

"Yes," Mr. Fricker asked, incredulous.

And I looked at him dead on, only realizing it that very second. "Yes."

It mostly started with a school play. To be exact, with sixteen-year-old Jim O'Reilly trying out for a part in *A Midsummer Night's Dream,* falling in love with a would-be gossip columnist he's known since kindergarten, and conducting a torrid, though anonymous, love affair with her (by e-mail).

How did he end up in a tree, his picture on the front page of newspapers all over the country?

And how did Jim O'Reilly get to be a shy, handsome romantic hero to millions of American girls?

———

His new love might be more interested in his twin brother, and his mom has just run away from home. But all this bad luck creates an amusing page-turner, with the reader dying to find out how Jim's life could possibly get any worse.

—*YM Online Magazine*

The plot becomes even more convoluted—and here comes the betrayal part—when Jim and Jake's mother suddenly leaves home, leaving Jim angry and confused. After a misleading spy session that makes it appear as if Mom is having an affair with a strange, unnamed man, readers learn that Jim's father is the one having the affair—with Jim's English teacher no less, who always does the costumes and scenery for the plays. There are so many twists and turns in this madcap story that Shakespeare surely would be proud. If it seems clear that the boy probably get the girl in the end, do not be so sure. He does, but which girl is another story."

—*VOYA, 2005*

As the story unfolds, Jim realizes that young love isn't always so innocent and pure. Cheating, secrets and lies abound amongst his friends and family. It seems that no one can keep it in their pants: Jim's mom leaves his dad, Zanny pledges her undying love to Jake while Jake's nympho girlfriend tries to hump anything with a pulse, and Gene's girlfriend dumps him for a guy she met on the Internet.

Colin Neenan writes about love in the grittiest of terms: love isn't easy, love sucks and love will mess you up, turn you upside-down and stomp on your brain until you can't see straight. Occurrences of drug and alcohol use, sex and unrequited teen love as seen from the male perspective, sprinkled with a healthy helping of humor, make this novella relevant to today's teens.

—*Curled up With a Good Kid's Book, 2005*